Dear Olly,

Also by Michael Morpurgo

The Dancing Bear
The Butterfly Lion
Farm Boy
Toro! Toro!

For younger readers

Albertine, Goose Queen
And Pigs Might Fly
Jigger's Day Off
Martians at Mudpuddle Farm
Mossop's Last Chance
Mum's the Word

Picture books

Sam's Duck
Wombat Goes Walkabout

Audio

Kensuke's Kingdom (read by Derek Jacobi)

Dear Olly,

MICHAEL MORPURGO

Illustrated by

CHRISTIAN BIRMINGHAM

TED SMART

This edition produced for The Book People Ltd,
Hall Wood Avenue, Haydock, St Helens WA11 9UL

First published by Collins in 2000
First published in paperback by Collins 2001
Collins is an imprint of HarperCollins*Publishers* Ltd
77-85 Fulham Palace Road, Hammersmith, London W6 8JB

The HarperCollins website address is
www.harpercollins.co.uk

1 3 5 7 9 8 6 4 2

ISBN 0 00 771835 7

Printed and bound in England by
Clays Ltd, St Ives plc

For Daniel Bennett

Dear Olly,

I have often thought of writing a story in movements rather than chapters – like a symphony. But for this I needed a story with three distinct yet linked themes, each with a different mood. Perhaps it was the moods and rhythms of the seasons that suggested this to me. And for me, it is swallows that are the magical conductors of the seasons.

I came across two stories that enabled me to compose my symphony story: one movement here, at home on the farm in Devon, one in Africa – and the two themes linked by a third, the swallow's flight from home to Africa.

I heard of a young Frenchman, so moved by the misery and horror of war and suffering in Rwanda that he gave up everything, and left at once to help in the only way he knew how.

Then, a good friend of mine suffered a dreadful car accident. Full of admiration, I watched how he coped with the pain, with the change it brought to his life. I charted his recovery, his rebuilding of himself.

Dear Olly, is a story about nobility and courage, courage against all the odds – the young Frenchman's, the swallow's and my friend's.

I hope you love reading it as much as I loved writing it.

MICHAEL MORPURGO
September 2000

Olly's Story

Olly was painting her toenails, light blue with silver glitter. She stretched out her legs and wriggled her toes. "What d'you think?" she said. She answered herself, because no-one else did. "Amazing, Olly, I think they're just amazing." But her mother and Matt had not even heard her. She saw they were both deeply engrossed in the television. So Olly looked too.

It was the news. Africa. Soldiers in trucks. A smoky sprawling city of tents and ramshackle huts. A child standing alone and naked by an open drain, stick-like legs, distended stomach, and crying, crying. A tented hospital. An emaciated mother sitting on a bed clutching her child to her shrivelled breast. A girl, about Olly's age perhaps, squatting under a tree, her eyes empty of all life, eyes that had never known happiness. Flies clustered and crawled all over her face. She seemed to have neither the strength nor the will to brush them off. Olly felt overwhelmed by a terrible sadness. "It's horrible," she muttered.

Suddenly, without a word, Matt got up from the sofa and stormed out, banging the door.

"What's the matter with him?" Olly asked. But she could see her mother was as mystified and as surprised as she was.

For some days now, she had known something was wrong with Matt. No jokes, no teasing, no clowning. He should have been on top of the world. Just a week or so before, his exam results had come in. Straight 'A's – he could go to veterinary college at Bristol just as he had planned. Olly's mother had been ecstatic. She had rung up and invited everyone to a celebration barbecue in the garden, spare ribs and sausages and chicken. They all expected, as Olly had, that sooner or later Matt would get into his clown gear and do his party act. But he didn't. He hardly said a word to anyone all evening.

Great Aunt Bethel, "Gaunty Bethel" as everyone called her, made a speech that took a long time coming to an end. "I just want to say well done, Matt," she said. "I know that if your father had been here, he'd have been as proud of you as we all are."

Olly never liked it when people talked of her father. Everyone else, it seemed, had known him, except her. To her, he was the man in the photo on the mantelpiece who had died in a car accident on his way to work one morning. She had no memories of him at all.

Gaunty Bethel had still not quite finished. "Now you can go off to college, Matt, and become a vet just like he was, just like your mother is."

Everyone had cheered and whooped and clapped, Olly as loudly as anyone, until she saw the look on Matt's face. He was hating every moment of it. It was true that just occasionally Matt could seem very far away and serious, lost in some deep thought. Olly knew well enough to leave him alone when he was like that. But this was quite different. He'd gone out in a fury, slamming the door behind him, and Olly wanted to know why. She went out after him.

She knew where she would find him. All summer the swallows had been flying in and out of their nest at the back of the garage. Matt had constructed a well-camouflaged hide at a discreet distance from the nest, and would sit in it for hours on end – he had done most of his exam revision up there – watching and sometimes photographing the parent swallows, as they renovated their nest, incubated their eggs, and now as they flew almost constant hunting sorties to feed their young. He never liked anyone to come too close when the swallows were nesting – he had even made his mother park her car in the street until the young had flown the nest.

Olly found him sitting up there in the hide, his knees drawn up to his chin. "Stay there. I'll come down," he said.

They walked together into the back garden. "They've hatched four," he went on. "One more to go, I hope." He sat down on the swing under the conker tree. It creaked and groaned under him. He didn't say anything for a while. Then he told her: "I've made up my mind, Olly.

I'm not going to college. I'm not going to be a vet."

"What about Mum?" Olly said. "What'll she say?"

"It's not Mum's life, is it? She wants me to be a vet because she is, because Dad was. Well, I don't want it. She just assumed I did. They all did. Ever since I was very little, Olly, I only ever really wanted to do one thing."

"What?"

"I just want to make people laugh. I want to make people happy. It's what people need most, Olly. I really believe that. And I can do it. I can make people laugh. It's what I do best."

Olly knew that well enough. Matt had kept her smiling all her life. Whatever her troubles – at school, with her mother, with friends – he had always been able to make them go away. Somehow he could always make her laugh through her tears. He had a whole repertoire of silly walks, silly voices, silly faces, particularly silly faces – he had a face like rubber. He could mime and mimic, he could tell jokes at the same time as he juggled – bad jokes, the kind Olly liked but could never remember. And when, on special occasions, Christmases, parties, birthdays, he dressed up in his yellow-spotted clown costume, with his oversized, red check trousers and his floppy shoes, painted his face and put on his great red nose and his silly bowler hat with the lid on it, then he could reduce anyone to gales of laughter, even Gaunty Bethel – and that was saying something. He could make people happy all right.

Matt wouldn't look at her as he spoke. "I'm going to be a clown, Olly, I mean a real clown. And now I know where I'm going to do it. I'm going where my swallows go. I'm going to Africa. Did you see that girl on the news with the flies on her face? There's thousands like her, thousands and thousands, and I'm going to try to make them happy, some of them at least. I'm going to Africa."

Everyone did all they could to stop him. Matt's mother told him again and again that it was just a waste of a good education, that he was throwing away his future. Olly said it was a long way away, that he could catch diseases, and that it was dangerous in Africa with all those lions and snakes and crocodiles.

Gaunty Bethel told him in no uncertain terms just what she thought of him. "What they need in Africa, Matt," she said, "is food and medicine and peace, not jokes. It's absurd, ridiculous nonsense."

Every uncle, every aunt, every grandmother, every grandfather, came and gave their dire warnings. Matt sat and listened to each of them in turn, and then said, as politely as he could, that it was his life and that he would have to live it his way. He argued only with his mother. With her, it was always fierce and fiery, and so loud sometimes that they would wake Olly up with it, and she'd go downstairs crying and begging them to stop.

Then one morning, when they called him down for breakfast, he just wasn't there. His bed was made and his rucksack was gone. He had left a letter for each of them on his bedside table. Olly's mother sat down on his bed and opened her envelope.

"He's gone, Olly," she said. "He's gone. He says he's taken out all his savings and gone to Africa."

Olly had seen her cry before, but never like this. She clung to Olly as if she would never let go. "I'm so angry with him, Olly," she said, and then: "but I'm so proud of him, too." It wasn't at all what Olly expected her to say.

Olly read her letter again, sitting up in the privacy of Matt's hide at the back of the garage.

Dear Olly,

I've got to go, I must. I don't suppose I'll write very often. I'm hopeless at letter writing, you know that. So don't expect to hear much. But I'll miss you a lot, I know I will. I'll tell you all about everything when I get back. Time passes very quickly. I'll be back before you know it. And don't worry about me. I'll watch out for all those lions and snakes and crocodiles, I promise. I'll be fine. Look after Mum for me. And look after my swallows too. Make sure they all fly off safe and sound before the winter comes. See you soon.

Love, Matt

Olly tried to do all he had asked of her, but none of it was easy. In those first days her mother was completely distraught. Olly kept telling her the same thing over and over again. "He'll be all right, Mum, he'll be all right, you'll see." It was all she could think of to say. But Olly didn't even believe it herself. Night after night she lay awake, sick with her own worry, and as sad as she'd ever been. Without Matt there was no laughter in the house any more, no joy.

She did make sure that nothing and no-one disturbed the fledgling swallows. Like Matt before her, she sat for hours at a time up in the hide, watching them, guarding them, shooing away any marauding cats. Day after day she witnessed the comings and goings of the parent birds, how they would swoop down to dive into the garage, and then flutter briefly at the nest, feed their young and be off again. Olly loved the sudden screeching chorus of excitement as the parent birds arrived, and the silence and stillness that followed. The young grew fast. Very soon the nest was impossibly full, full of beaks, gaping beaks.

Then one day, as Olly climbed up the ladder into the hide, she saw they were not there. They had flown. She found them lined up on the garage roof waiting to be fed. She could watch them better from her bedroom window now. It wasn't long before the five fledglings were quite indistinguishable from all the other swallows and swifts and martins soaring and screaming around the chimney pots on a summer's evening.

In all this time there had been no word from Matt, no address, nothing. Olly's mother was fretting herself to a frazzle. Olly tried to reassure her that no news must be good news. They speculated endlessly, where he might be, what he might be up to, whether he was all right.

There was a succession of unwelcome

visits to endure. Gaunty Bethel came round almost every other evening. If she could, Olly would escape to her room and hide, but sometimes there was no avoiding her. Gaunty Bethel was so loud, so opinionated, so judgmental. "If you ask me," – and no-one had, of course – "I put it down to the schools, the teachers. Children come out of school these days thinking the world's their oyster. Not like it was, I can tell you. When I think, Olly, of all your mother has done for that boy, brought him up practically single-handed and then he just ups and goes off like that. And to Africa! To be a clown! What is he thinking of? It's just not right, not responsible, plain thoughtless. I don't know" – and then came the pained sigh – "I don't know. Young people these days."

These were difficult times for Olly.

She was missing Matt more than she ever thought possible. She found herself alone in the house more than ever – there was always some crisis at the surgery that meant her mother was having to work even longer hours than usual. She went often to Matt's room and sat on his bed. She felt closer to him there, but it didn't help. It made it worse if anything. She went round to see her friends, but they were holiday happy and she wasn't. So that made her miserable too. Sometimes, to cheer herself up, she would go out on call with her mother, to carry her "bag of tricks" as she called it – her bag of medicines. They went to the bird sanctuary to mend a swan's wing, to a dairy farm to help with a difficult calving – a breech birth. But once back in the car, talk would soon turn to Matt, and one or other, or both of them, would always end up in tears.

It was three weeks to the day since Matt left that the cards arrived, one each, from Rwanda. Olly read hers over and over again, soaking in every word. His writing was tiny, as always, and very difficult to read.

Dear Olly,

I finally got here. I'm working in an orphanage run by Irish nuns and nurses. Sister Christina is the boss nun. She's over sixty, but you wouldn't know it. I've never seen anyone work so hard. She never stops. There are over two hundred children here. I help feed them and teach them, and every evening I do my clowning show and try to send them to bed happy. Some of them find going to sleep very difficult – not surprising when you think what they've been through. One of the boys, Gahamire, doesn't speak at all because he's been so frightened. I want to help him speak again if I can. From my window, I can see a big mountain with clouds around the top. They say lots of gorillas live up there. Haven't seen one yet though.

Lots of love, Matt

P.S. Did my swallows fly?

The card to Olly's mother said more about the orphanage, about the plight of the children, how undernourished and weak some of them were, how terribly wounded – some without legs after stepping on landmines. He gave no address. He just said he would write again. They put their cards on the mantelpiece either side of the silver framed photograph of Olly's father and, for a while at least, Matt's cards were enough to lift the gloom about the house.

Olly went off to school for the new term with a spring in her step. The dark rings of anxiety under her mother's eyes all but vanished. Now both of them could at least picture the place where Matt lived, and what he was doing. One evening, they took out the atlas. Olly's mother remembered a film she'd seen about a mountain in Rwanda where gorillas lived. She worked out it must be somewhere in the Virunga range, near Lake Kivu. So now they knew roughly where he was. All of this helped, for a time; but then fresh doubts and anxieties began to surface once again.

"Why didn't he leave his address?" Olly asked. "Then we could write back to him."

"Maybe he just forgot," her mother replied. In their hearts though, both of them knew the real answer. Matt wanted to do what he was doing alone, without them. He's flown the nest, Olly thought, like the swallows in the garage, he's flown the nest and gone. Sometimes, when she was feeling sad, she even hated him for it, but never for long. It was hard, hard for her and her mother, but at least they knew that Matt was alive and safe and well; and as time passed, and they became more used to his absence, they found they could be glad for him that he was at least doing what he wanted.

Then Olly came back from school one afternoon and noticed a swallow flying in and out of the garage. She climbed up into the hide to get a closer look. There was another swallow sitting on the nest. So once again Olly's mother found her car banished to the street, and once again whenever she wasn't at school Olly found herself on guard duty up in the hide. She took her mug of tea with her. She even did her homework there sometimes.

To begin with, it was because she knew Matt would have wanted her to do it. But the more she watched them the more she became absorbed in their lives. She loved their elegant agility in flight, their dogged perseverance, and their faithful and total devotion to their young. Always reluctant to leave her swallows, she had to be bullied and pestered and cajoled to come in for supper each evening. She was very careful to remove the ladder each time she left the hide, just in case there was a cat on the prowl. And if she ever saw a cat anywhere nearby, she would turn terrier and chase it off.

This time there were only three fledglings, three yellow beaks peeking out of the nest – such ugly, scrawny-looking birds to start with, Olly thought, and then, so soon, sleek and blue and beautiful. Olly wanted to be there this time, to see the moment they flew. Each morning she checked the nest before she left for school, and every afternoon she raced home from school and up the ladder.

She was sitting up there in the hide one September afternoon when her mother came home from work. "Haven't they flown yet?" she asked from outside the garage. "They'd better hurry. They'll need to be on their way south very soon now. It'll be October next week. You tell them. Then come in for your tea."

Olly stayed with them for a few moments more, willing them to fly, and then telling them to as well. "You've got a long way to go, d'you hear me? Africa. It's thousands of miles away. That's where Matt is. You can't just sit there feeding. You've got to get going."

She left the fledglings gazing back at her, beady-eyed and blinking. She ran inside, downed her tea in a few gulps, picked up a sticky bun and a packet of crisps and was out again within minutes. Two of them had already flown and were now up on the garage roof, side by side and begging to be fed. She checked in the nest. The last one would fly at any moment. Determined not to miss the moment, she waited and watched. He was perched on the edge of the nest, hopping about, flapping his wings, but he wouldn't take off, he wouldn't fly. No matter how much Olly willed it, he just would not fly.

Some time later, her mother called her in again, for supper. Olly protested, but it was no use. Her mother was adamant. She sat her down in the kitchen and made her eat a proper meal. When Olly ran back into the garage, a large black cat shot out right past her. She had left the ladder up. The nest had been completely destroyed and lay scattered on the ground. The last fledgling was nowhere to be seen. She found him, eventually, wings spread out and still as death, behind a watering can in the darkest corner of the garage. Olly gathered him into her hands and rushed indoors.

The kitchen instantly became a casualty ward, her mother deft and calm as she examined him under the light. Olly stood by the sink, crying in her grief and remorse.

"Well, his wings aren't broken and there's been very little bleeding," said her mother after a moment or two. "I think he's just stunned, traumatised. I'll be honest with you though, Olly, his chances are still not very good. I'll give him a few drops of glucose to get his strength back, and then all we can do is keep him warm somewhere, and just hope he'll recover."

The glucose seemed to have no effect whatsoever. They laid him down in a cardboard box close to the stove, and Olly sat over him and watched him. Only his eyes moved. Sometimes, it appeared he was looking directly up at her, and their eyes would meet. Olly stayed with him all evening, sitting by the box, hoping, praying. She wanted to stay up all night, but her mother wouldn't allow it.

"Worrying over him won't help, Olly. We've done all we can. You've got school tomorrow." And she took her off to bed.

Quite unable to sleep, Olly crept downstairs in the still of the night. The swallow had not moved. She reached in and stroked his head with the back of her finger. "Come on," she whispered. "Live. Please live." Her mother found her by the box an hour later, fast asleep, and led her up to bed where she slept heavily for the rest of the night.

Olly was woken suddenly. "Olly! Olly! Come quickly!" Olly took the stairs in threes. Her mother was standing by the stove. She had the swallow in her hands, and she was laughing out loud. "Isn't it wonderful?" she cried. "He's just raring to fly. You can feel the strength in him. You know what we'll do, Olly. We'll put a ring on his leg before we let him go. It won't take a second. It won't hurt him. Then we'll know him when he comes back next year, won't we? Have a look in my bag of tricks. There's a packet of rings in there I keep for the bird sanctuary. It's in there somewhere, I know it is."

Olly rummaged in the bag and found what she was looking for. The ring was slipped on in a trice – a bright scarlet ring.

The two fledglings were still perched on the garage roof, as Olly had hoped they would be, the parent birds swooping overhead. Olly fetched the ladder and held it fast while her mother climbed, very gingerly, one hand on the ladder, one holding the swallow. At the top, she reached out and set him down on the ridge, harried all the while by two very agitated parent birds. The rescued fledgling fluttered his wings, scratched himself and shifted along at once to join his two siblings.

"A proper little hero," said Olly's mother as she stepped down off the ladder. "That's what he is, a proper little hero." They stood back to watch and admire.

"Hero. Hero. We'll call him Hero," said Olly. "The perfect name for him."

When at last one of the parent birds flew down and fed him, Olly and her mother hugged each other in triumph.

And when some minutes later he took off, flew across the drive and landed safely in the cherry tree, they cheered him all the way.

Hero stayed about for a few weeks. Olly watched him avidly as he learnt the whole repertoire of swallow acrobatics: diving, swooping, skimming, hovering, twisting, turning, gliding, soaring. Through binoculars, Olly could sometimes still spot her scarlet-ringed swallow amongst the dozens of swallows now lining up on the telephone wire. She often thought she saw him – a young swallow on his own – out of her classroom window, swooping down to drink from the puddles in the play-ground, or sitting perched on the wall by the school gate. She hoped it might be him, but he was too far away for her to be sure and she knew it probably wasn't.

Then one afternoon, on her way home from school, she saw that there were no swallows any more on the telephone wires, none skimming over the cricket pitch, none playing chase amongst the chimney pots. They were gone. Hero had gone. It left Olly feeling very empty and very alone.

"He'll come back. Most of them do, you know," said her mother that night when she came in to say goodnight to Olly.

"You think so? You really think so?"

"We'll look for him next spring, next April. Fingers crossed."

"He'll be going where Matt is, won't he? To Africa," said Olly. "Maybe they'll meet up, you never know."

"Do you know what I wish?" her mother said, sitting down beside her. "I wish I was a swallow, just like Hero. I'd fly all over Africa till I found Matt."

"And I'd go with you," said Olly.

Hero's Story

Hero joined the others as they flocked to a nearby lake, and for several days he hunted there, skimming over the water after midges and mosquitoes. He was safe here with his family, in amongst the thousands upon thousands of milling swallows and martins; and all the while his strength grew within him. At dusk they gathered to roost in the trees and reed beds around the lake. Every night in the roost the air of expectancy grew. Every night the birds were slower to settle to their silence and their sleep.

Then one morning, early, the hobby falcon came gliding high over the lake. They heard his killer *kew-kew* call and

scattered
in terror.
Down came
the hobby,
swifter than
any bird Hero
had ever seen.
Hero felt the wind of
him as he passed by,
and swerved aside only
just in time. But the hobby
was not after him, he was
after a young martin, slower
and more stuttering in flight than
Hero – and for the martin there
was no escape.

The flock flew that same morning, a spontaneous lift off, swirling out over the lake, a whispering cloud, darkening the sky as it went. They wheeled south, south towards the sea, hoping they had seen the last of the hobby falcon. But the hobby was not far behind, for he too was bound for Africa. He would fly all the way with them, picking off the youngest, the slowest, the weakest, whenever he felt like it. He had done it before.

Out over the coast of France he struck once again. Hero knew, as they all knew, that they must stay together, stay close and never fall behind. They flew high, where they could see the danger, where the flying was easier anyway, where they could float on the warm air. But they had to come down to drink, to feed, and that was when the hobby falcon pounced. He would appear in amongst them out of nowhere, wings cutting through the air like scythes, shadowing them, stalking them. He took his time, but once the hobby falcon had singled out his prey, there could be only one outcome. No amount of fancy aerobatics could deceive him. He would simply follow, close and kill. He was remorseless, tireless, merciless. There was always a strange sense of relief when he had killed – the survivors knew they were safe, then, for a while at least.

On they flew, on over the vineyards,

on over the mountains.

It was evening over Spain, and the air was heavy with a gathering storm. The birds tried to rise above it, but the storm was suddenly upon them and could not be avoided. They bunched as they flew into it, desperately seeking each other's shelter, but were scattered at once by a whirling wind that whipped them about the blackening sky. Hero found himself alone. Lightning flashed and crackled all around him. Pounded by the rain and by hailstones, too, Hero dived earthwards, faster now in his fear than he'd ever flown

before. Still the storm was all around him, still he could not see the ground. Then, below, a glow of sudden light, some small hope of escape. But Hero found that his sodden wings would not beat as they should. He was falling like a stone – down, down towards the light. He could only spread his wings wide, willing them to take flight again. When at long last they did, he found himself floating down into the pool of light, a light dazzling bright and full of noise. But Hero was not afraid. He was out of the storm and that was all that mattered.

It was a football stadium. He sought out a convenient perch, the crossbar of the goalpost, settled and fluttered the wet from his wings. Here he would rest.

The goalkeeper looked up at him and laughed. "Hello, friend," he said. "Stay as long as you like. I'll be doing my best to see you're not disturbed, but I can't guarantee anything."

Hero knew that he could not rest for long, that all the while the flock would be moving further away, would be more difficult to find. He had to go, and go now. He fluffed up his feathers and shook himself ready. At that moment, the television cameras found him and focused on him. There he was – a giant swallow – up on the big screen.

Twenty thousand voices cheered him as he took off and flew, up out of the light into the darkness beyond.

Even in the black of night, even without the others to guide him, Hero sensed in which direction he must go, where south must be. But he could not know where his friends were, how far away, nor how high they would be flying. Hero heard the storm still rumbling overhead. He would fly low, low and fast, and just hope to find them at first light. It was the dread of losing them, of being left behind altogether that gave new power to his wings.

All night long Hero flew, but as the sun came up and warmed his back he saw he was still quite alone. He fed constantly on the wing, and the feeding was good, the flies fat and plentiful.

There was water whenever he needed it, which was often. It was as he was drinking, as he was skimming the blue stillness of a mountain lake, that he felt a sudden cold shadow pass over him. He saw the reflection in the water below. The hobby falcon! He shrieked in his terror and tried frantically to gain height and speed, twisting and turning to avoid the talons outstretched just above him, ready to snatch him from the air. One claw ripped a feather from his back, but did not touch the flesh. Then Hero was up and away, climbing towards the sun. But the hobby falcon came after him, his wing beats stiff and strong.

Now, Hero's only chance lay in his agility, and in his ability to deceive his enemy in flight. For sheer speed the hobby falcon would have the better of him.

He feinted, he weaved, he dodged – but the hobby was always still there, right behind him, and waiting for just the right moment. For hour upon hour the chase went on over the parched high sierras, along lush river valleys, in amongst the roofs and chimneys and aerials of hilltop villages and towns.

Hero was tiring, and tiring fast now. There was a forest below filling the valley. He saw his one last chance. With the hobby still on his tail, he dived

suddenly down in amongst the shadows of the cork trees. He flitted through the branches, flashed through the dappled light, seeking the darkest depths of the forest. A glance back, and then another. The hobby was nowhere to be seen. On he sped, just to be sure, to be very sure. His eyes scanned the forest about him. The hobby had not followed him. He had lost him. He was safe at last. He landed, his heart beating wildly, and perched there for some time, on the lookout all the while for the stubby-tailed silhouette he so much dreaded, listening for the killer *kew-kew* call he never again wanted to hear.

Hero had stayed long enough. He had to go, he had to risk it sometime. He lifted off his perch out of the dark depths of the forest and flew away south, straight as an arrow, high over the sunlit sierras.

The hobby came down on him like a bolt from the blue, missing him by only a whisker at the first pass, so close Hero could see the dark glint in his eye. The bare sierras stretched away to the horizon – they offered no hiding place. Hero dived, and the death shadow followed him. He cried out, steeling himself for cruel claws that would tear the life out of him.

A gunshot blasted the air about him.

Hero saw the hobby stagger and stutter in flight, and hurtle to earth, where he bounced and bounced, and then was still. Hunters came running over the hills with their dogs.

Hero could feel the wind off the sea ahead, and the heat of the desert beyond, beckoning him on. The sea was quickly crossed. He drank from a swimming pool, beside a hotel of white marble, in Morocco. Children were playing there, laughing with delight every time he came swooping down to dip into the blue of the water beside them. But once the children had gone inside, once he had drunk and fed his fill, Hero set off across the desert. He flew by the moon, by the stars, keeping low over the sand.

The great red sun came up over the desert and chased away the cold of the night. Still no water, still alone. Hero cried out for his friends again and again as he flew. *Tswit. Tswit. Tswit.* Never an answering call, never a sign of them. All day and another night and another day, Hero flew, gliding, resting on the thermals whenever he could, for he felt his strength ebbing away fast. Without water he could not go on much longer.

And now there came a hot desert wind blowing against him, slowing him. He saw the billowing sandstorm in the distance, and heard its dreadful roaring. To be caught in it would be certain death. He would have to fly over it. With the very last of his strength he beat his way skywards. Try as he did, Hero could not entirely avoid the stinging lash of the fringes of the storm, but at least the murderous heart of it had passed safely beneath him.

Hero glided now because there was no power in his wings to do anything else. He was completely exhausted. That last stupendous effort had finished him utterly. He floated on the air as far as he could. He called out desperately for his companions. *Tswit. Tswit. Tswit.* Suddenly, the whole desert seemed to be answering him. He called again, and from the heat haze below came a clamouring chorus of welcome. The haze darkened and became trees – an oasis of palm trees amongst the sand dunes below him, where every tree was alive with birds, all of them singing out their greetings.

Hero floated down to join them. They were there in their thousands, swallows and martins, and swifts, too. Hero landed where he needed to, right at the water's edge. It didn't matter a bit to him when a camel came down to drink beside him. Camel and swallow drank together, oblivious to anything but the sweet cooling relief of the water.

When Hero had finished his drinking, he bathed himself, dunking himself again and again, and then preening his feathers clean. He had a feast of flies that evening too, before he settled to roost in the trees, amongst his family, the smoke of the Tuareg fires all about them.

Morning brought the sound of Tuareg children playing around their tents, and Hero fluttered down to watch – he liked to be near children. Camels chewed and groaned and grunted nearby, and Hero fed hungrily on the flies that hovered over them. As the Tuareg knelt to morning prayer, they heard the call of departure sounding through the oasis,

then the murmur of thousands of shivering wings as every swallow and every martin and every swift lifted in unison out of the trees and swirled southwards and away out over the desert.

Another day, another night, and they left the desert behind them. Below them now were the first scrubby trees, here and there a village, and then the wide grassy plains of Africa, waterholes and rivers and great lakes. Here they could feed and drink as they went. Here, everything seemed plentiful. There were great herds of wandering wildebeest drifting over the

plain below, loping giraffes as tall as the trees, leaping impala, slumbering lions, elephants browsing, wallowing, trumpeting, and new birds that made new sounds.

Then, from somewhere below him in amongst the trees, Hero heard the sound of excited voices and a sudden squawking. Several swallows peeled off the flock and drifted down to investigate, and Hero went with them. Here was a solitary baboon squatting on a rock, here a herd of zebras startled into a snorting stampede, and all the while the babble of shouting voices and that strident squawking. Hero flew on so entranced by it all, so intrigued, that he had not even noticed that he was alone. He swooped down through the canopy of the trees, down towards the voices, down towards the squawking.

The net, a giant parrot trap, was stretched from tree to tree right across the clearing. Hero did not see it until he flew into it. He fought to extricate himself, but his leg and his wing were caught fast. The more he flapped and struggled the more he became entangled. He cried out in his pain and terror. *Tswee, Tswee. Tswee, Tswee.* Below him and above him, hanging there in the net like Hero, hopelessly enmeshed, were several small grey parrots and one larger, brightly coloured parrot that squawked louder than all the others. The hunters were hauling down the net, plucking out the parrots they wanted to keep and stuffing them into their sacks. Hero was grabbed, tugged and twisted, and at last wrenched free of the net, before being thrown aside like so much rubbish.

He was quite unable to move. A few metres away from him, and lying in the long grass, was the scarlet ring. It had come off in the struggle. As the bird hunters finished their business, Hero drifted into unconsciousness. When he woke the world was silent and still about him. His leg hurt him terribly, but he could hop on the other one, with the help of his wings. That was when he saw the

cobra, poised above him to strike, puffing himself into a fury. Hero flapped away frantically, half hopping, half flying. The cobra's first strike missed. By the second, Hero was airborne and well out of danger. He found he could manoeuvre only clumsily, but he managed to fly up through the trees, up towards the open sky. Once there, he cried out for help, cried out for his companions. But he was alone in an empty sky, and completely bewildered. He had no idea where he was, nor where he should go.

He was driven by one powerful compulsion, simply to keep going for as long as he could. For many days he flew on, deeper and deeper into the heart of Africa, stopping ever more frequently to rest his damaged leg. Landing was difficult for him. He could perch on only his one good leg. The crushed claws on his left leg hung loose and useless. But he could drink, he could hunt, and he could fly.

Early one morning, as Hero was flying over lush mountainsides, skimming the treetops, he found himself suddenly lost in a blinding mist. He flew down, and after several false attempts, landed at last in amongst the dense foliage of the jungle. There was a stream below to drink from and all the insects he could wish for. He sat on lookout, until he was quite sure it was safe, and then dropped down to the stream to drink. He was in mid-flight when he heard a thunderous pounding close by, and then a great crashing in the undergrowth. Hero flew up in alarm and perched to watch.

A massive silverback gorilla was coming down to drink, and he was followed by his entire family. Afterwards, they settled down right below him to do their grooming – grunting and groaning contentedly – until at last they all fell asleep in a huddle, all except the silverback, who went and sat on his own some way off. Hero called to him. *Tswit. Tswit*, and the silverback looked up lazily and considered him for a while with his great brown eyes, before he dozed off.

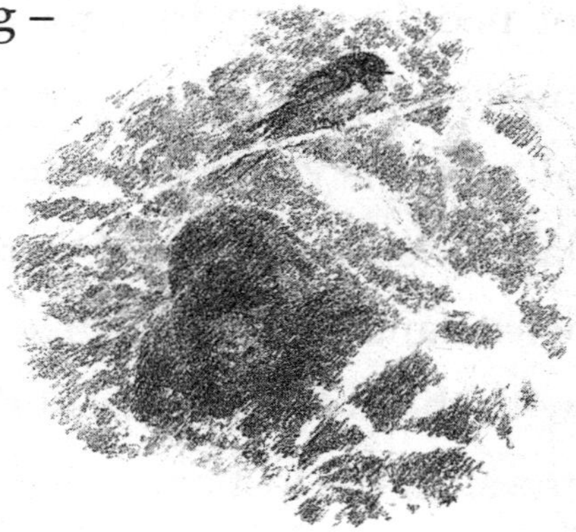

Later in the day, the sun lifted the mist off the mountainside and Hero flew away over the mountain. On the far side was a broad valley and a dark lake beyond. The smoke of many fires rose into the air from the valley floor. He flew lower. People, thousands upon thousands of people living in a ramshackle city of huts and tents, a refugee city, spread out all over the valley from the foothills to the lakeside, a place of wretchedness, a wasteland of human misery that echoed with the howling cries of the hungry and the sick, the lost and the grieving.

Hero flew out over the lake to feed, and the feeding was easy – for it was almost evening by now and the flies were down. He dipped down to drink and, as he did so, he heard from some way off a sound he knew so well – the sound of children's voices. As he left the lake behind him, Hero saw below him a courtyard of long low buildings, and there were children laughing. They were all sitting on the ground, watching a clown, a clown in a battered bowler hat, red check trousers, a yellow spotted jacket, and floppy shoes. He was juggling and tripping over his feet at the same time, staggering about, almost dropping the balls, but never quite. The children were squealing with joy.

Hero landed and perched on the courtyard wall and looked on. The balls were going higher and higher and higher, and then, one by one, the clown made them disappear until there was only one left. This one he popped into his mouth and swallowed, licking his lips and rubbing his tummy with delight. The children cheered and laughed, until he hushed them to an attentive silence. Then he crouched down and began to tell them a story. As he did so another swallow came down to join Hero on the wall, and another and another, until the whole wall was lined with them. Hero knew at that moment that he had flown as far as he would go. He had all he needed here. He had arrived.

The children listened open-mouthed in wonder as the clown finished his story. He lifted his battered hat and bowed to them. They clapped and begged for another. It was then that the clown looked up and noticed the swallows. "Look!" he cried, pointing straight at Hero. "Look, children! Swallows. You see those birds up there on the wall? They're swallows."

Two hundred heads turned and looked. "They've come a very long way, children," the clown went on. "Some of them perhaps all the way from England, from my country. All those thousands of miles just to see you. Now that's something. That's really something, isn't it?"

Matt's Story

There was thunder about the mountain that evening, and the children were uneasy. They would be difficult to settle. Matt was hot in his clown costume, but he didn't mind. The courtyard had rung with laughter as he'd told them his story of the Sultan and the Cockerel – their particular favourite – and that was all that mattered. The new girl, just brought in that morning – Matt couldn't remember her name – sat cross-legged at his feet, beaming up at him. She had gappy teeth, and Matt remembered Olly being like that, and all the business of the tooth fairy. Home seemed a million miles away, on another planet. The swallows on the wall reminded him that it wasn't.

Evenings were when Matt really came into his own. He was busy enough by day about the orphanage, working alongside Sister Christina and the dozen or so nurses and nuns, helping out wherever he could – in the kitchen, cleaning down in the dormitories and the hospital, sometimes teaching under the tree in the courtyard.

In the few months he had been there Matt had become the great fixer, their handy handyman. As Sister Christina once told him teasingly: "You understand all the truly important mysteries of life, Matt – generators, Land Rover engines, wiring, plumbing, drains." Matt had made himself quite indispensable about the place. And he had never been so happy. For the first time in his life he felt completely fulfilled at the end of each day. Dawn to dusk, he worked his heart out and loved every moment of it. But dusk was best. "Matt's happy hour", as Sister Christina called it, or "Funny Man time", to the children.

And so it was, an hour of clowning antics and joking and juggling and story-telling in the court-yard before the children were taken off to their dormitories for the night. Settling two hundred children to sleep is difficult at the best of times, but as Matt was discovering daily, all these children had lived through unimaginable horrors and terrors, and the coming of night seemed to be the time when their memories returned to haunt them, the time they most missed their mothers and fathers.

For Sister Christina, too, and for everyone who worked at the orphanage, "Matt's happy hour" had become the one time of the day they could all look forward to. No-one liked to miss it. They laughed because they rejoiced to see the children so happy and bright-eyed, but also because Matt somehow managed to touch the child in each of them as well. Day in, day out, they were dealing with children so wounded in body and soul, that it was sometimes very difficult for them to keep their own spirits up. To them "Matt's happy hour" was manna from heaven, a blissful haven of fun at the end of the day. They loved him for it, as did the children, and for Matt the warmth of that love meant everything.

With the story over, the children drifted slowly across the courtyard to their dormitories. Matt had one on his back and half a dozen more clutching on to his hands, his arms, his baggy red check trousers, in fact anything they could hang on to.

He helped settle them into their beds, cuddling where a cuddle was needed, whispering goodnights, calming fears. As he had expected, it took longer than usual that evening for the air was heavy and humid. But that was not the only reason. That afternoon they had heard an explosion. It was some way away – probably another landmine, Sister Christina had told him – but close enough to send a shiver of apprehension through the orphanage. All the children knew well enough what such sounds meant, and what horrible damage such sounds could do to the human body.

Matt came at last to Gahamire's bed. He was sitting up, waiting for Matt as usual. Gahamire grabbed him by the hand and pulled him down beside him. He snatched off his battered bowler hat,

put it on, mimicking one of Matt's sad faces and then bursting into laughter.

The transformation of Gahamire had been dramatic and wonderful. Only two months before he would do nothing but sit and stare vacantly at Matt as he clowned and frolicked in the courtyard. He would spend all day sitting on his own, rocking back and forth, never speaking a word to anyone. Then one day, as Matt was flat on his back under the Land Rover changing the oil, he felt someone squatting down beside him. It was Gahamire. Matt reached out and touched his nose with an oily hand, and Gahamire's face cracked into a smile. "Funny Man," he said, and he'd stayed to watch.

Since then, Gahamire had latched on to Matt, and would never go to sleep at night until he had been to say goodnight to him. Matt had a whole routine.

"We'll do gorillas again, shall we?" said Matt. Gahamire nodded and waited. "Well," Matt went on, "you know where they live, don't you? On the top of that mountain. They're up there now, going off to sleep just like you. We'll go up there one day and see them, shall we? And how does the big gorilla say goodnight?"

Gahamire beat his chest and the two

of them made gorilla faces at each other and giggled.

"And how does the big gorilla scratch himself?" Gahamire rolled on his back on his bed, and grunted and groaned and scratched himself.

"And how does the big gorilla pick his nose?" And Gahamire stuck his finger up his nose and wrinkled up his face in disgust.

"And how does the big gorilla go to sleep?" Gahamire snuggled down at once and closed his eyes.

"Night, night, big gorilla," said Matt, and he got up to go. But Gahamire still had him firmly by the hand and wouldn't let him go.

"What is it?" said Matt.

"My home. My home is by a mountain, a big mountain," said

Gahamire. "I go. I go up the mountain to find my mother."

"Of course you will, Gahamire. Sleep now."

Matt was strangely restless that night. His thoughts rambled and raced. He thought of the swallows again on the courtyard wall, of the nest in the garage at home, of Olly, of his mother. He should write more often. They'd be worrying. He'd write a card tomorrow. He thought of Gahamire, and wondered if his mother could possibly be alive. So far as anyone knew, both his parents were dead. Such happy reunions did happen. Not often, but they did. He fell asleep, smiling in the hope of it.

It was at breakfast that they discovered Gahamire was missing. As the others were searching through the compound, Matt made his way to the Land Rover, got in and drove off. Sister Christina called after him. "Matt! What are you doing? Where are you going?"

"To the mountain. He's gone to the mountain. I'll find him." He roared out through the gates and was gone up the dusty track before anyone could stop him. Matt was quite sure of it. Hadn't Gahamire told him he would go looking for his mother? And like an idiot, hadn't he dismissed it as mere wishful thinking?

He took the most direct route to the mountain, the way he thought Gahamire must have gone, across the road and up the steep rutty track beyond. Here, he stopped the Land Rover, turned off the engine and called out. There was no reply, only his own echoes dying in the trees all around. Ahead of him the mountain rose steeply on either side of the track, thickly wooded all the way up. He couldn't see the top as the whole range was covered in a blanket of mist. Matt drove on slowly, his eyes peeled, stopping every now and again to call for him, to listen for him. "It's me, Gahamire. It's Funny Man. Are you there? Are you there?"

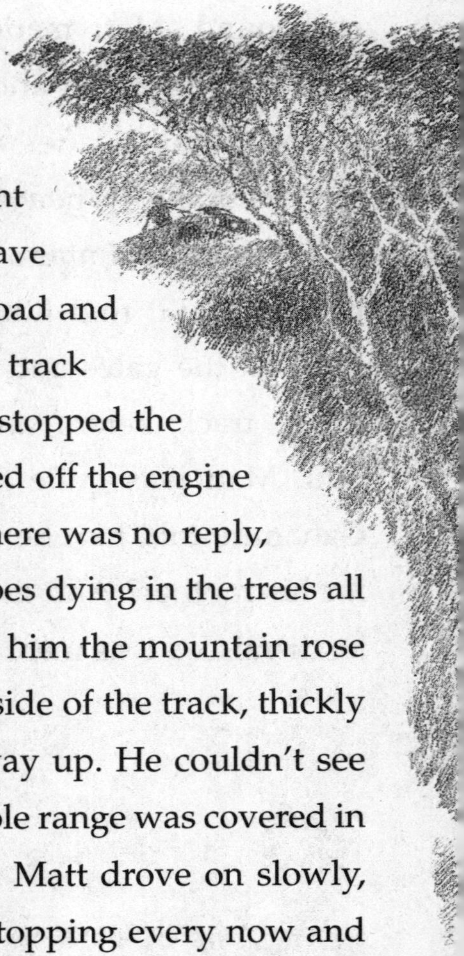

For an hour or more he drove on like this, stopping and calling, and starting again. But still no voice answered him. And then, out of the corner of his eye, a sudden shiver of movement. Matt stopped the Land Rover. A shadowy face, then eyes, wide white eyes in amongst the trees. He had found him.

He turned off the engine. Gahamire was cowering in the undergrowth, rocking back and forth and moaning, his face wet with tears. Matt approached him slowly, talking as he came. "It's all right, Gahamire, it's only me. It's Funny Man."

Gahamire looked up at him. "The men, they come to my village. They kill and they kill. My mother hid me under the altar in the church. Then she went away—"

But Matt never heard the rest of what Gahamire said, for that was the moment the landmine exploded under his foot.

Matt came to consciousness only a few moments later. His head was full of pain and noise. He tried to sit up, but couldn't. Gahamire's face seemed to be swimming in amongst the trees above him. Matt couldn't decide if Gahamire was wailing or humming. He couldn't work out what he was doing lying there.

"I'd better get up," Matt said. But Gahamire held him down hard by his shoulders. "You stay still, Funny Man. You stay still." Matt tried to fight him, but he seemed to have no strength. He felt himself being swirled away down into a murky darkness and wondered if he would ever wake up again.

When he did, some hours later, he was in the Land Rover. He knew the smell of it, the sound of it. He felt no pain, only bewilderment. All about him was a haze of faces and voices. Then Sister Christina was talking to him. Her voice sounded far away.

"Matt. Matt. You're going to be all right." Gahamire was beside him, holding his hand. "Don't you worry,"

Sister Christina was saying. "We'll have you in hospital in just a jiffy. It's the French hospital. It's not far."

It was the look on Gahamire's face that told Matt it was serious. He panicked then and struggled to raise himself to see what he could, but Sister Christina held him fast where he was. It took all her strength to do it. She tried to calm him, to reassure him. Only then did it occur to Matt that he might be dying. "You'll tell my mother?" he said. "You'll tell Olly?" Then he knew nothing more.

When he woke, he could feel a dull ache in his leg. He was covered in a white sheet. There was a nurse at his bedside.

"Hello Matt," she said. She spoke in a heavy accent. "I will fetch the doctor for you."

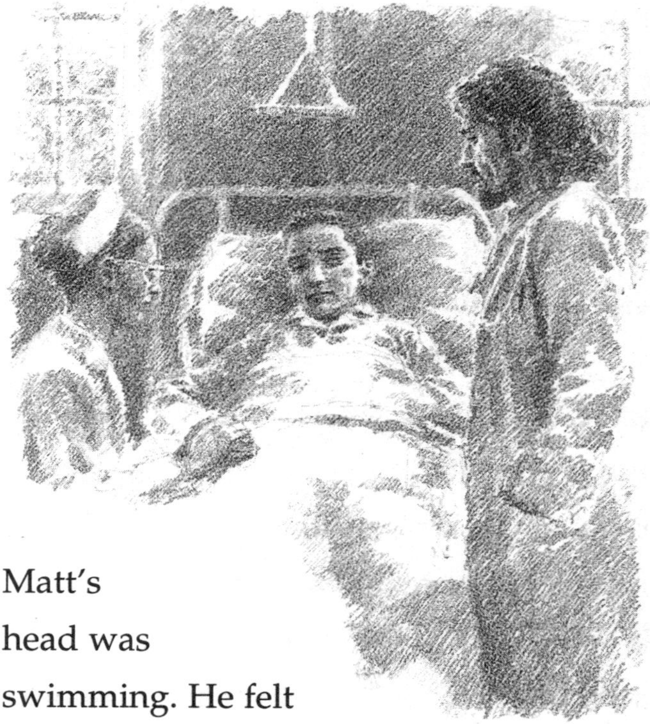

Matt's head was swimming. He felt himself drifting off to sleep.

When he opened his eyes again the doctor was standing by his bed. He had long black hair and a beard. Matt thought he looked like a pirate. The nurse took his hand and held it, and Matt wondered why. The doctor spoke almost perfect

English, but he seemed uneasy. "You came through the operation very well. How do you say it? Strong as an ox? You'll be up and about in ten days."

"What's the matter with me?" Matt asked. "What happened?"

"A landmine," the doctor said. "I have to tell you, Matt. Your right leg. We did all we could, but I'm afraid we could not save it. It's not so bad, Matt. They'll make you another one, not so good as before, maybe, but you'll be able to get around, do what you want, live a full life. It will take time, though."

"But I can wriggle my toes," said Matt. "I can feel them."

The doctor crouched down. "I know you can, but it's not real, it's in your head. I'm very sorry, Matt."

"And my other leg?" Matt asked. "Is

my other leg all right?"

"It's fine," said the doctor. "Everything else is fine. You had a bump on the head. So you've got a wonderful black eye, that's all."

They gave him morphine to keep the pain down, and for days Matt lay there drifting in and out of sleep, woozy even when he was awake. He found it difficult to remember anything at all clearly. Sometimes he was awake when Sister Christina brought Gahamire in to visit him. If he was, then they would play draughts together, or just talk for a while, or Gahamire would ask for a story or a trick or a funny face, and they'd laugh. It was so good to laugh. And when he became tired, Gahamire would know it and climb on to his bed and sleep with him, his head in the crook of Matt's arm.

Now, he spoke often to his mother on the phone, and to Olly. He could hear

they were trying their best not to cry. They were unreal to Matt, like voices from a dream. They asked lots of questions, all of which came down to the same thing: "How are you?"

Matt had thought it out already. He was very firm about it on the phone to his mother. "I don't want Olly to see me, Mum, not yet, not till I'm ready, not till I'm up on my feet again." She said she understood, that she'd explain it to Olly, that she'd be there to meet him at the airport, and would take him to the hospital in London where he could recuperate, where he could have his new leg fitted.

When the time came for Matt to leave the hospital, the ambulance took him on a short detour back to the orphanage, so that everyone could say their goodbyes. The whole place had been decked out with flags and bunting, and everyone was singing: *For he's a jolly good fellow.* Then Gahamire came up and presented him with his battered bowler hat. "You come back, Funny Man," he said. And Matt found he could neither answer nor smile. All he could do was wave. Then they closed the ambulance doors and drove him away to the airport.

Alone in the aeroplane, Matt cried at last – for his lost leg, and because he was being torn away from the orphanage, from Gahamire and the children, from the place and the people who had made him so happy.

As she had promised, his mother was there at the airport to meet him. There were tears, of course, but Matt made her laugh in the end. "It'll be cheaper on shoes and socks, Mum," he quipped. "Come on, cheer up. It's only one leg. I've still got the other one."

Once in Roehampton Hospital in London, there were endless weeks of convalescence to endure. Matt's bedside was surrounded with cards and flowers, and with more grapes and kiwi fruits and peaches than he could eat in a lifetime. And there wasn't a day when he didn't have a visitor. But each day seemed like a month to Matt. Although the doctors seemed pleased enough with his progress, he was not. The healing was slow, so slow.

Matt passed his time by writing letters, some to the orphanage, and every day to Olly. Every letter to her ended with a promise that she could come and visit soon – just as soon as he was up and about and walking on his new leg – or "Peg" as he now called it. In every reply – and she replied to every single letter and spoke to him often on the phone – Olly begged to be allowed to see him. But it was two long months before she finally received the letter she'd been waiting for.

Dear Olly,

Peg is a strange creature, but I'm really beginning to get used to her, even to like her in a funny sort of way. She's a bit skinny – not the right word really – compared to my other one, but there are some advantages – not many, I admit, but it's one leg less to wash in the bath and I don't have to cut so many toe nails! It's weird – sometimes I can really feel my old leg, my former leg, my previous leg. Honestly. Sometimes I want to scratch it. My stump still gets sore, which is a real pain, but it's better every day now.

Like I told you, I promised myself I would be on my two feet and walking, no crutches, no wheelchair, before you saw me. Well now I am. So you can come up and see me if you want to. We'll go for a walk on Putney Heath – that's just down the road. There's a hot-dog stand there with sausages as long as cucumbers and lovely dribbly, juicy onions. And they've got the creamiest ice-cream I've ever had. How about it? I had another letter from Gahamire yesterday with a picture of two giraffes nose to nose. They look as if they're kissing. I'll show you. See you soon.

Love, Matt

Matt was ready and waiting for Olly when they came up to see him a couple of days later. The steps outside the hospital were difficult, but once down on the grass he walked towards her with scarcely a limp, just as he had promised himself he would. He was leaning slightly to one side perhaps and he still needed his stick, but for Matt it was the most triumphant walk of his life. He even managed to stay on his feet when Olly threw herself into his arms.

When all the hugging was over and done, the three of them went to sit down on a bench in the spring sunshine and feasted on hot dogs. Afterwards, he introduced Peg to Olly. "Well, Peg," he said, "this is my little sister. You can kick her whenever you like. Have a look, Olly." Olly lifted up his trouser leg to look. "See?" Matt went on. "She's a lot nicer than my other one. No horrible hairs."

Shortly after this, Matt came home at last. He didn't want any fuss, he said, no grand welcome. So they kept it all very quiet. But in those first days back home, the visitors, mostly relatives, came and went almost constantly. Matt clowned his way through it all – it was the only way he could deal with it. Gaunty Bethel was particularly horrified when Matt rolled up his trouser leg to show her. "Love me, love my Peg," was one of his lines. And then his worst joke of all, "Meet the new bionic Matt, a leg-end in his own lifetime." He could see Olly was uncomfortable with his black humour. In one of their quieter moments he did try to explain it to her. "If I didn't laugh about it, Olly, I'd cry. And I'm telling you, I've done enough of that for a lifetime."

Matt had imagined the worst of it was over, but it wasn't. Back in the hospital everyone had had one limb or another missing. No-one had been any different. But now, every day, he had to endure the averted eyes, the hushed admiration, the endless sympathy.

Gaunty was the worst. "If I hear her telling Mum just once more how wonderful I am," he told Olly, "I'll bop her with my crutches. Honestly I will."

He so much wanted to live a normal existence again, and to forget about his leg, but it wouldn't heal quickly enough to let him. He hated the exercises he had to do for hours every day to strengthen his muscles. He knew they had to be done, but he loathed every minute of them. There were doctors' visits, nurses' visits and the dreaded trips back to hospital for check-ups as an outpatient. None of this helped Matt to forget. He began to sink into sadness. He even stopped writing to the orphanage. It pained him even to think of the life he'd had to abandon. He felt himself giving up, losing interest, giving in to despair, and he could do nothing about it.

Olly was the only one he really wanted to be with because she treated him just as she always had. He walked her to school each morning – with a stick to help him, he could just about manage it there and back – and was often there to meet her when she came out. They were on their way back home one afternoon when Olly first noticed the swallows flitting about over the treetops.

"Look, Matt, they're back! They're back!" she cried. "Maybe Hero's come back, too. Oh I hope so, I hope so."

Matt knew all about Hero – Olly had told him the story again and again,

and he understood just how much Olly had been looking forward to his return.

"We'll get the garage ready for him," Matt said. So once more, the car was banished to the street.

But in the days that followed no swallows came to the garage, although there were plenty about. Everyone was on constant lookout for Hero, for a swallow with a scarlet ring. Matt busied himself in the evenings making a ladder with broader steps so that he could get himself up into the hide and be there when Hero came back. And so Matt and Olly were there in the hide when a pair of swallows did fly into the garage and begin to build again in the very same place as the year before. But neither had a scarlet ring. Matt tried his best to soften the bitterness of Olly's disappointment.

"Perhaps he's just gone somewhere else," he said, and he told her again about the swallows he'd seen flying around the orphanage back in Rwanda and how they had reminded him of home. "I came home, didn't I?" he said. "So will Hero. You'll see."

The nest grew by the day, a meticulous miracle of a nest, the parent birds dipping down into muddy puddles, flying in and out, building incessantly. Matt was up there almost all day, every day, watching, guarding, photographing. The eggs hatched and the begging beaks appeared, four of them. For Matt, this was the first time since his accident he could lose himself in something completely. When he was up in his hide he was able to forget his leg entirely. With every passing day now he grew stronger. He felt the shadows of despair lifting, and was more and more at peace with himself.

One afternoon, he turned up to meet Olly at school, for the very first time with no walking stick, his eyes bright with excitement. "Well?" he said, holding out his arms and pirouetting proudly.

Olly played at being unimpressed. "So you can walk on two legs," she teased. "What's so great?" Then she hugged him tight. "Clever Peg," she said. "Clever you."

"There's something else I've got to tell you and it's even better," Matt went on. "Come on, I'll show you when we get home."

He took her at once up into the hide. "Watch," he said. "Keep your eye on that one, the father. You watch him when he perches." It was some time before either of the parent birds took a rest from feeding the young. When at long last one of them did, Matt whispered, "You see? The father bird, he can't use his right leg. Look at him. He's like me."

"So?" said Olly.

"Well, he manages, doesn't he?" Matt went on. "One leg or not, he's flown all the way here, and come the autumn he's going to fly all the way back again. And that's just what I'm going to do. I'm going back, Olly, back to Africa."

"Not for a while, please," said Olly.

"Not for a while, Olly," he replied. "Not till the swallows fly."

Thanks to Bean & Nick

C.B.

"Mobility is a human right;
mobility is a birthright."

The Jaipur Limb Campaign is working in partnership with the Mozambique Red Cross Society and has set up a rehabilitation centre in Gaza Province to help people who have lost limbs because of landmines. The JLC is also supporting four organisations in India to build rehabilitation centres and provide professional training for more staff to help people who have lost limbs and who are suffering from the effects of polio.

A donation has been made by HarperCollins Publishers to the Jaipur Limb Campaign, in recognition of its important work.

For more information, contact the
Jaipur Limb Campaign, 11 Goodwin Street,
London, N4 3HQ
020 7272 9501 (tel), 020 7272 9544 (fax)

THE BUTTERFLY LION

by Michael Morpurgo

Bertie rescues an orphaned white lion cub from the African veld. They are inseparable until Bertie is sent to boarding school far away in England and the lion is sold to a circus. Bertie swears that one day they will see one another again, but it is the butterfly lion which ensures that their friendship will never be forgotten.

"The Butterfly Lion is unique among animals and books, and will touch all hearts – both young and old."

Virginia McKenna, Born Free Foundation

Winner of the Smarties Prize and the Writers' Guild Award.

Collins